HERGÉ

THE ADVENTURES OF TINTIN

THE SECRET
OF
THE UNICORN

METHUEN CHILDREN'S BOOKS

LONDON

Translated by Leslie Lonsdale-Cooper
and Michael Turner

The TINTIN books are published
in the following countries :

Argentina :	JUVENTUD ARGENTINA,	Buenos Aires
Australia :	HICKS, SMITH & SONS,	Sydney
Belgium :	CASTERMAN,	Tournai
Brazil :	DISTRIBUIDORA RECORD,	Rio de Janeiro
Canada :	METHUEN,	Toronto
Denmark :	CARLSEN/IF,	Copenhagen
Egypt :	DAR AL MAAREF,	Cairo
Finland :	OTAVA,	Helsinki
France :	CASTERMAN,	Paris
Germany :	CARLSEN VERLAG,	Reinbek-Hamburg
Great Britain :	METHUEN,	London
Greece :	PEGASUS,	Athens
Iceland :	FJÖLVI,	Reykjavik
Indonesia :	INDIRA,	Djakarta
Iran :	PAT MARTY,	Teheran
Israel :	MIZRAHI,	Tel Aviv
Italy :	GANDUS,	Genoa
Japan :	SHUFUNOTOMO,	Tokyo
Mexico :	MARIN,	Mexico
Netherlands :	CASTERMAN,	Utrecht
New Zealand :	HICKS, SMITH & SONS,	Wellington
Norway :	SCHIBSTED,	Oslo
Peru :	DISTR. DE LIBROS DEL PACIFICO,	Lima
Portugal :	CENTRO DO LIVRO BRASILEIRO,	Lisbon
Singapore :	BOOKS FOR ASIA,	Singapore
South Africa :	HUMAN & ROUSSEAU,	Cape Town
Spain :	JUVENTUD,	Barcelona
Sweden :	CARLSEN/IF,	Stockholm
U.S.A. :	ATLANTIC -LITTLE, BROWN,	Boston

First published in Great Britain in 1959
Reprinted 1965, 1968 and 1971
Published as a paperback in 1974
Reprinted 1975
Printed by Casterman, S.A., Tournai, Belgium
ISBN 0 416 80020 3

THE SECRET OF THE UNICORN

NEWS IN BRIEF

AN alarming rise in the number of robberies has been reported in the past few weeks. Daring pickpockets are operating in the larger stores, the cinemas and street markets. A well-organised gang is believed to be at work. The police are using their best men to put a stop to this public scandal.

We must keep our eyes open, and catch these crooks.

How about starting in the Old Street Market? Tintin said he was going there this morning. Perhaps we'll meet him.

Good idea. Let's go.

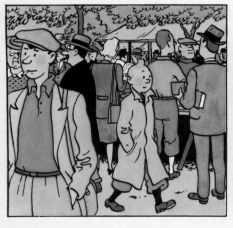

Why, there are Thomson and Thompson.

Hello! ... How are you?

Look who's here!

Tintin!

What are you doing here? Looking for bargains?

Sh!...Highly confidential!... Special operation: pickpockets.

But that didn't stop us from finding this job-lot of walking sticks. ...

How much?

A pound for the lot.

Sixty pence!

Eighty...but I'm robbin' meself...

What's going on?

They caught some thieves red-handed.

Special Branch! Special Branch!... You can tell that to the Inspector!

Snowy!... Snowy!

All right, I'm coming...

I say. Snowy, isn't that a fine ship!

It really is a beauty. I've a good mind to buy it for Captain Haddock....

How much?

A quid. It's a unique specimen. It's a very old... er... very old type of galliard.

Eighty pence!

Done! Yours for eighty pence.

How much is that ship?

Sorry, sir. I just sold it to this young gent.

!

I'll buy it from you.

I'm sorry, sir, but it's not for sale

Look here, young fellow, I'm a collector... How much did you pay? I'll give you double for it!

Thanks, but I'm keeping it.

How much is that ship?

I'm sorry, sir, but this ship is not for sale.

Look. I'll give you a fiver for it!

A tenner!

NO!

Twenty!

Thirty!

Look here: I want to give this ship to a friend of mine. I'm not selling it, so please don't pes - ter me any more!

Now why were they both so keen to buy my ship?

A few minutes later...

It really is superb... Captain Haddock will be delighted.

RRRING

I expect that's him...

I apologise : it's me again!

?

Forgive me if I am too insistent. But as I explained, I'm a collector - a collector of model ships. And I would be so very grateful if you would agree to sell me your ship.

I've already told you, I bought it for a friend...

Exactly! Now I have other ships just as good as yours, and we could exchange them so that your friend...

It's no good. Please don't go on. I'm keeping it.

Very well. But think it over. I'll give you my card, so that if you change your mind...

I shouldn't count on it!

Well, I shall hope.

Goodbye, sir.

CRASH

?

What's happened?

Snowy!... What have you done?

Look, now it's broken!

Luckily it's not too bad. I can soon mend it.

RRRRING

This time it must be the Captain.

Hello!

Hello, Captain. Just the person I wanted to see.

Come on in. I've got a surprise for you.

Tintin, what a magnificent ship!

Thundering typhoons!

Where... where did you find this ship?

In the Old Street Market... Why?

Ten thousand thundering typhoons!... What a remarkable coincidence!... Imagine!...

No! Come with me: then you'll see!

Remarkable!... It's really remarkable!

Here we are! Now ...

You'll see ...

Look!

Is ... is that you? ...

No, it's one of my ancestors, Sir Francis Haddock. He lived in the reign of Charles the Second.

But just take a closer look at that ship in the background...

It's just like the one you saw in my room, isn't it?

Exactly!... It's the same ship!... It's identical!... Don't you think that's remarkable?

There's a name here. Look there, in tiny letters: UNICORN

So there is: UNICORN. I'd never noticed it.

Maybe there's a name on mine too... We should have brought it along. Wait here: I'll go and fetch it.

If mine has the same name, that'll really be funny...

Let's see ...

Great snakes!... It's gone!

You are mistaken, young man. I've had this ship for more than ten years!...

Ten years? But you were trying to buy it from me less than two hours ago!

This wasn't the ship!... Not this one!... Yours was, in fact, exactly the same, but it wasn't this one!

Indeed?...

Well, sir, we can soon tell. Just after you'd gone, my ship fell over and the mainmast was broken. I put it back, but you can see where it broke. So we'll look at your mainmast, if you don't mind!

It's not broken!... This isn't my ship!

So, you see!

I can understand your surprise. I myself was amazed to find an exact replica of my own vessel in the Old Street Market. And because it seemed so odd, I did all I could to persuade you to part with it...

Please do forgive me, sir... I am so very sorry...

That's all right! And if you find your ship, let me know

It's extremely odd! Two ships exactly like the one in the Captain's picture... and with the same name: UNICORN.

I must telephone the Captain at once: He'll be amazed!

Engaged!

It really is unbelievable how long people can chatter on the telephone! More than a quarter of an hour! Ah, at last!

We can go now, Fifi: it has stopped raining...

No reply : the Captain must have gone out. We'll go home . . .

As for my burglar, it must have been the second man who tried to buy the ship . . .

My door's open ! . . . What can be the matter now ? . . .

My flat has been ransacked ! . . .

The gangsters ! What have they done to my books !

This one is completely ruined ! . . . The vandals !

Burgled twice in one day . . . Not bad at all !

What have they taken this time ?

Very queer thieves : they haven't taken a thing.

They've only searched the place . . . I wonder what they were looking for ? . . .

Next morning . . .

9

Hello. How are you?...
Good heavens! Whatever's happened?

Er... nothing really... just a little spot of bother, in the Old Street Market..

Er... yes... a slight mis-understanding. Anyway, we've come to pay you the money for those sticks. We called last night, but you were out.

Did you get your wallet back all right?

I'm afraid not. But I bought a new one this morning, and ... and...

Goodness gracious! I've been robbed again!

! !

Great Scotland Yard!... That man we met last night on the stairs, on our way here!... I remember now: he bumped into me!...

What was he like?

He bumped into me, too!

Quite tall... coarse features ...black hair... small black moustache... blue suit... brown hat...

That's him... the man from the Old Street Market!

But he couldn't have stolen your wallet last night, when you only bought it this morning.

There's something in what you say...

Miserable thieves! A brand new wallet! Come along, Thomson, we must report this right away!

He's right!... We must report it at once...

Look out!

Hey, Thompson, wait for me. Where are you?...

Here!... I'm downstairs already!

Poor old Thomsons, they do have rotten luck!... There seems to be quite an epidemic of larceny and house-breaking.

Oh well, let's try and get these papers sorted out...

What are you after, Snowy?

A cigarette, under there? That's a funny place...

Why, it's not a cigarette... it's a little scroll of parchment...

But this isn't mine! Where ever did it come from?... Let's have a closer look at it...

Here's another mystery!

But it's all gibberish! And where on earth did this parchment come from, anyway?

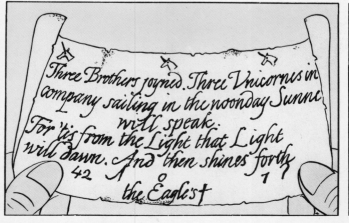

Three Brothers joyned. Three Vnicornes in company sailing in the noonday Sunne will speak. For 'tis from the Light that Light will dawn. And then shines forth the Eagle's †

42   1

Avast, pirates! Avast there! Captain!...

Avast, you dogs!... Sea-gherkins!... Baboons!

Buccaneers!... Fili-busters!.. Bagpipers!... Gallows-Fodder!

We've won!... That's got them on the run! ...With a yo-ho-ho and a bottle of rum!

What's all this play-act-ing for?

Play-acting?...This isn't a play!... Come in, and you'll understand ...

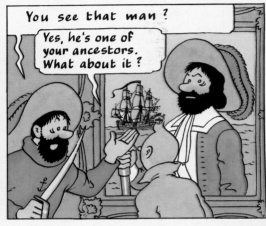

You see that man?

Yes, he's one of your ancestors. What about it?

Well, last night, when I was thinking about this strange business of the ships, I suddenly remembered that up in the attic I had an old sea-chest belong-ing to my ancestor. This is it ...

In the chest I found this hat and cutlass, and also...

I know! Treasure!... Or a treasure-map!

No, not treasure, but something like it!... Old manuscripts by Sir Francis Haddock... Look, I started reading them yes-terday evening, and read all night...

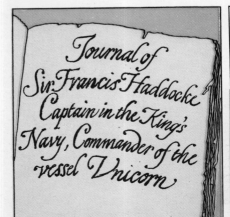

Journal of Sir Francis Haddocke Captain in the King's Navy, Commander of the vessel Unicorn

I was still reading when you came in. That's why you found me a little... over-excited. But what a story! Just listen to it!

It is the year 1676. The UNICORN, a valiant ship of King Charles II's fleet, has left Barbados in the West Indies, and set sail for home. She carries a cargo of... well, anyway, there's a good deal of rum aboard...

Two days at sea, a good stiff breeze, and the UNICORN is reaching on the starboard tack. Suddenly there's a hail aloft...

Sail on the port bow!

Thundering typhoons!.. She's mighty close-hauled! Ration my rum if she's not going to cut across our bows!

And she's making a spanking pace! Oho! she's running up her colours.. Now we'll see...

!

Got her!

Got her, yes! But not a crippling blow. The pirate ship in turn goes about - and look! she's hoisted fresh colours to the mast-head!

The red pennant!... No quarter given!... A fight to the death, no prisoners taken! You understand? If we're beaten, then it's every man to Davy Jones's locker!

The pirates take up the chase - they draw closer... and closer... Throats are dry aboard the UNICORN.

Close hauled, the enemy falls in line astern with UNICORN, avoiding the fire of her guns ... She draws closer...

Then suddenly, not more than half a cable's length away, she slips from under the UNICORN's poop...whoosh, like that!

Then she resumes her course. The two ships are now along-side. The boarders prepare for action ...

Here they come! Grappling irons are hurled from the enemy ship. With hideous yells the pirates stream aboard the UNICORN.

All hands to repel boarders!

Stand back! Out of my way! Can't you see the pirates swarming over the side!

Back, you dogs!

Back, you rats! Avast, sea-lice! Belay, lubberly scum!

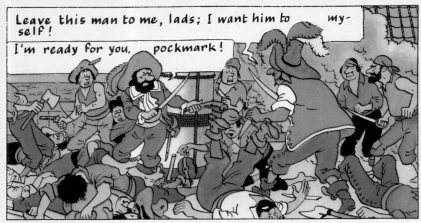

Leave this man to me, lads; I want him to myself!

I'm ready for you, pockmark!

You'd like to kill me, eh gherkin? Scoffing braggart!

Saucy tramp! So, you'd kill me, would you?...

There! Take that, centipede!

Oh, so you'd attack me from the rear, would you, cowards?...

Then look out for squalls!

Well, that's more or less what happened to my ancestor. As he hurled himself on the pirates, a heavy block drop-ped on his head, and he fell to the deck, stunned.

The pirates were masters of the ship. They had hoisted the red pennant - and they gave no quarter. Every man jack walked the plank...

And Sir Francis?

Sir Francis?... When he came round he found himself securely lashed to his own mast. He suffered terribly...

From that blow on the head, of course...

No, from thirst!...

Poor man, how he suffered.

He looked about him. The deck was scrubbed, and no trace remained of the fearful combat that had taken place there. The pirates passed to and fro, each with a different load...

What's happening? Instead of pillaging our ship and making off with the booty, they're doing just the opposite.

But there's a man approaching. He wears a crimson cloak, embroidered with a skull: he's the pirate chief! He comes near - his breath reeks of rum - and he says:

Regard me well, dog: I am Red Rackham!

Your servant, sir. And I am Sir Fra- -ncis Haddock.

Doesn't my name freeze your blood, eh? Right. Listen to me. You have killed Diego the Dreadful, my trusty mate. More than half my crew are dead or wounded. My ship is foundering, damaged by your first attack, then holed below the waterline as we boarded you...

...when some of your dastardly gunners fired at point blank range. She's sinking...so my men are transferring to this ship the booty we captured from a Spaniard three days ago.

And what booty!

Look at these diamonds!

These are worth more than six times a king's ransom . . .

Did you come here just to tell me that ?

No, that's not why I came. I came to tell you that those who annoy me pay dearly for their folly ! Tomorrow morning I shall hand you over to my crew. And that flock of lambs know just how to administering ter a lingering death !

So saying, he laughed sardonically, picked up his glass and drained it at a gulp, like this . . .

That's enough, Captain! Go on with your story . . .

Very well . Towards nightfall, the UNICORN with her pirate crew sighted a small island. Soon she dropped anchor in a sheltered cove . . .

Darkness fell; the pirates found the UNICORN's cargo of rum, broached the casks, and made themselves abominably drunk . . .

Abominably! . . . Yes abominably . . . that's the word . . .

Hey, what's the idea? . . . I only wanted to show you . . .

You don't have to, I quite understand.

Just as you like, Tintin . . . Now where was I ?

The pirates were abominably drunk . . .

AAAAA-AAAAH !

That's funny! Now there are two glasses!

Well, in the meantime...

In the meantime Sir Francis struggled desperately to free himself...

Just you wait, my lambkins! Ration my rum if Sir Francis Haddock doesn't soon give you something to remember him by...

Done it! That's one hand free!

Free! Now I'm free!

On your guard, Red Rackham: here I come!

And with these words he hurled himself...

On the pirates?.. Like that?... Unarmed?...

No, on a bottle of rum, rolling on the deck!... He opened it, put it to his lips, and ...

And then he stops. "This is no time for drinking," he says, "I need all my wits about me". With that, he puts down the bottle...

Yes, he puts down the bottle... and seizes a cutlass. Then, looking towards the fo'c'sle where the drunken roistering still goes on...

You sing and carouse, little lambs!... I'm off to the magazine!

23

You know, of course, the magazine in a ship is where they store the gunpowder and shot...

There!... The party won't be complete without some fireworks!

Now I must make haste! There's just time for me to leave the ship before she goes up!

So, I've caught you!

!

So, dog, you'd blow us sky-high!... Well, you won't have that pleasure! I'll skin you alive, be- fore I even douse that fuse!

By Lucifer! I'll shave your beard, porcupine!

And I'll pluck those feathers, squawking popinjay! Fancy-dress freebooter! Fresh-water pirate! Pithecanthropus!

Retreat as you may, you cannot escape me!

I'll run you through, prattling porpoise!

And as he fought, Sir Francis kept thinking of that fuse, about to touch off the powder at any moment...

Suddenly, nimbly parrying a thrust, he leapt to one side...

With one swift blow from his heel he extinguished the fuse!

WOOOAH!

Now, Red Rackham, my temper's rising!

BANG
THUMP
ZZINNG
CRACK

Victory! Red Rackham lies dead! With a yo-ho-ho and a bottle of rum!

That's that! May heaven forgive your wicked soul!

Enough delay! Now to light another fuse...

...and be off!

No one has seen me: they're still drinking. Quick, into the jolly-boat...

Jusht look at the j-jolly-boat... [sh...ish going away...

Nonshensh! You're sheeing shings... you'sh drunk...

Hurrah! Justice is done!

So perished the UNICORN, that stout ship commanded by Sir Francis Haddock. And of all the pirates aboard her, not one escaped with his life...

What happened to Sir Francis after that?

He made friends with the natives on the island, and lived among them for two years. Then he was picked up by a ship which carried him back home. There his journal ends. But now comes the strangest thing in the whole story...

On the last page of the manuscript there is a sort of Will, in which he bequeaths to each of his three sons a model - built and rigged by himself - a model of the very ship he once blew up rather than leave her to the pirates. There's one funny detail: he tells his sons to move the mainmast slightly aft on each model. "Thus," he concludes, "the truth will out".

That's it, Captain!... Red Rackham's treasure will be ours!

What's the matter? OOOH!...

Ooooh! Lord love us! It's Mr. Sakharine... Someone's murdered Mr. Sakharine!...

?

Dead?

No, he's alive: his heart's beating. He's been chloroformed...

Tintin, look there! The second UNICORN... and the mast's broken!

Look! The foot of the mast is hollow: the parchment has gone!

Thundering typhoons! We aren't the only ones hunting for Red Rackham's treasure!

Don't move, anyone!

Ah, my old friends! I...

I'm sorry. We're on duty. On duty we can have no friends!

Quite right! We're here to clear up this business...

First, here's the victim...

To be precise: here's the victim!

Now, if there's a victim, there must be a culprit.

A brilliant deduction! Now we only have to find him... and he can't be far away. To be precise: he isn't far away...

In fact, there he is!

Me, the culprit? You dare accuse me?... Miserable earthworms!.. Sea-gherkins!

Slave-traders!.. Sea-lice!...Black-beetles!...Baboons!

Artichokes!...Vermicellis!... Phylloxera!... Pyrographers!

Crab-apples!... Goosecaps!... Gogglers!... Jelly-fish!

Captain! Captain! Calm yourself!

Yes, please calm yourself, Captain. We only said that by way of an experiment...

What sort of experiment?

You see, if you really had been guilty, you'd have been upset. As it is, we are now quite convinced of your innocence.

Now, to work! We must look for fingerprints.

Goodness gracious!...The corpse has gone

Look!...Your corpse is coming round!

What happened to you, Mr Sakharine?

A man came here last night, to offer me some fine old engravings. As I bent over to look at them I felt a pad clamped over my nose...

No doubt it was chloroform, for I became unconscious...

Very odd...To be precise... Can you smell something burning?

Your magnifying-glass! Ha! ha! ha!... your magnifying-glass... and the sun!... Ha! ha! ha!..

Stop laughing in that stupid way! Try to concentrate on the case.

Can you describe the man who came to offer you those engravings?

Wait... I seem to have seen him before ... but I can't tell where...

He was rather fat. Black hair, and a little black moustache. He wore a blue suit, and a brown hat.

That's him!... That's the man in the Old Street Market!

What man in the Old Street Market!

A man who tried to buy the ship I found in the Old Street Market. You know him too: he's the one you met on the stairs on your way to see me last night. You suspected him of stealing your wallet ...

By the way, do you know mine has been stolen too?...

No! It's extraordinary how many people let their wallets be stolen! It's so easy not to... Here, you try and take mine...

Go on, try!...

It's on elastic!

Simple enough... If you only think of it!

Childishly simple, in fact. But now we must leave you to your investigations. Goodbye ...

Goodbye.

If things go on like this, Red Rackham's treasure will disappear from under our noses...

Yes, I'm afraid so...

Look, someone seems to be waiting for us outside my door...

The man from the Old Street Market!

Mr. Tintin?...

Yes. What can I do for you?

I'd like a word with you, please Mr.Tintin. But not here, if you don't mind. It would be quieter in your flat...

All right. We'll go up...

In you go...

BANG BANG BANG

Bandits! Crooks! Gangsters!

Captain! Captain! Help me!

Take care!... They... they will kill you... too...

Who?

Who?... Who are they?... Tell us...

There... ?

Sparrows?... What do you mean?... Crumbs, he's fainted!...

Ah, Captain!... Come with me...

Where?..

To see the Thomsons: they've found my wallet!

There's no mistake: it's mine all right.

He had seven in his pockets. The day's takings, no doubt.

?

Here's the parchment from the UNICORN's mast. Look, Captain...

Er... that's good...

Tell me: how did you manage to catch the thief?

Catch him?!... Well, to be quite honest, we only managed to catch his morning-coat.

Yes, it's certainly a morning-coat. How odd for a pickpocket to wear a thing like this.

Isn't it?

The trouble is that the coat doesn't give us any clue about its owner's identity...

Doesn't it?

Look at these stitches; they make up a number. That means the coat has been to the cleaners recently.

Goodness, you're right!

So... to find the thief's name and address, we've only got to trace the cleaners who use this mark. Quick, we'll make a list of cleaners from the telephone directory, and start hunting for the thief at once!

CLEANERS

Some days later...

Mr. Tintin?
The first floor.

All right? O.K., O.K.

Mr. Tintin? Here's the dinner service you ordered.

Me? I haven't ordered anything.

But it's addressed to you... Look...

Right! the chloroform's done the trick. Quick, shove him in the crate.

Wait: I'll shut the door.

WOOAH!
WOOAH!

Wasn't Mr. Tintin in?

Yes, but there's some mistake. He hadn't ordered anything.

That confounded tyke's at the window!

WOOAH!
WOOAH!

Hello, Snowy! What's the matter?

Snowy!... Snowy!... Be careful! You'll fall!

The dog's gone crazy: look at him chasing that van.

It's funny: he never leaves his master, as a rule.

Is Mr. Tintin upstairs?

Yes, he's in.

Mrs. Finch!... Mrs. Finch!... Tintin isn't in his room!

Not in?... Then where can he be?

Next morning...

Where on earth am I?

It looks very much as if I'm a prisoner...

Yes, a prisoner!

36

Nobody there! But I wasn't dreaming: someone spoke!

Yes, someone spoke!

Who... who are you?... And where are you?

Who am I? I am the ghost of the captain of the UNICORN!

Ha! ha! ha! ha! ha!

Ha! ha! ha!... That frightened you, didn't it?... Come over to the door... Come on.

Come nearer. Good... Now, can you see the speaking-tube?

Who are you, and what do you want with me?

Who am I?... You must allow me to remain anonymous... And why did I have you kidnapped? You have guessed that, no doubt...

I want to know where you have hidden the two parchments you stole from me.

Me? I stole two parchments?... But I never had more than one.

Come on now, let's be sensible! I'd collected two of the three scrolls: you took them from me. That night when I had your flat searched, only the third one was found... in your wallet. Where are the other two?

How should I know?

As you like. But I warn you: I know of several ways to loosen stubborn tongues... I'll give you two hours to tell me where you hid those scrolls, then if you won't talk, you'll soon see the sort of man I am!

But I tell you... Oh he's cut off, the gangster!

Now I'm in a fine mess! How do I get out of this one?

Two hours!... Two hours to get out of here!... How can I do it?

I wonder if I could use this beam as a battering-ram, against the door...

Hopeless! I can hardly lift it...

No good. But in two hours I must be miles away...

Eureka!

First I'd better block up this speaking tube with my handkerchief

Then no one will hear any noise I may make...

Now to work! As fast as I can...

First I'll knot these sheets and blankets together...

Then tie them securely to this beam...

And pull!... Heave-ho!... Heave-ho!... Heave-ho!... Heave!...

Start again: I've simply got to move this beam. Now...

Meanwhile...

A quick bath and I'll soon get rid of this mud.

Aha! It's good to be nice and clean again.

That's it: there's the beam under the ring.

Now I'll tie a small stone to the end of this string, like this ...

Whoops!

And that's made a fine battering-ram!

Now then, here we go!

WHAM

Did you hear that?

Yes, a muffled thud. It shook the whole house.

There it is again ...

That's odd ... Sounded as if it came from the cellars ...

BOOM

From the cellars? But ...

By thunder! It must be Tintin. I expect he's calling us - to tell us where those scrolls are hidden ...

Hello? ... Hello Tintin? ... Hello? ... Hello? ... That's funny: he's not answering ...

But the noise is going on.

We must get to the bottom of this. Come with me; we'll see what's happening.

BOOM

40

It's coming from the cellars all right.

Now, one last go: the wall's cracked already, so...

Hooray, there she goes!

CRASH

It's a musical-box! It fell over, and started to play!

There he is!

Over there... By thunder, he's rammed a hole through the wall!

Stop!... Stop!... Little devil, he's bolted!

See him?... There are plenty of hiding places here. But we'll get him.

Careful! We must be on our guard...

There! That armour... it moved!

So, my friend, you thought you'd be smart and hide in a suit of armour. Well, you're caught: come on out!

You won't? That's too bad for you! I'll count up to three and then I fire. One... two... three...

BANG
BANG

DONG

!

Confound it! He wasn't inside the armour!

Did you hear that?

Yes, it's nothing. A bullet ricocheted off the armour and struck that gong over there. Come on, don't let's waste time...

Whew! What luck! ...They've gone past. I'll just slip out...

Where are they? I can't see them...

CUCKOO!

CUCKOO!... CUCKOO! ...CUCKOO!

Stupid! That's not Tintin: it's a cuckoo-clock striking. Come, let's get on with it.

On you go, Tintin! You're in luck!

!

42

Whew! I just saved it in time!

BOOM

This time it's Tintin... We've got him now.

He can't be far off...

There he is!... Stop!... Stop!... or I'll shoot!

BANG BANG

A counting-frame!... that gives me an idea...

CRACK

That was a good idea . . .

Little devil! He'll pay dearly for this . . .

So sorry to have to leave you, gentlemen . . .

And now, tough guys, it's your turn to be locked in . . .

No time to lose. I must have these gangsters arrested at once.

!

Now I see what he meant- the man who was shot- pointing to the birds. He was giving us the name of his attackers! ... Just look at this letter ...

Messrs. M. + G. Bird, Antique Dealers, Marlinspike Hall, Marlinshire, ENGLAND.

Quick, let's ring up the Captain ...

Hello... yes... it's me... yes... Who's speaking? What? Tintin!... I... Where are you? Hello?... Hello?... Hello?... Hello?... Are you there?...

What am I doing here?... I... er... I'm Mr. Bird's new secretary. Didn't you know that?...

I... no, I hadn't heard. Please excuse me, sir.

Hello, Nestor!... Nestor!...

Hello, Nestor!... A young ruffian's broken into the house! Stop him telephoning his accomplices! We're coming at once. Don't let him get away, whatever you do!

Hello, Captain! I'm at Marlinspike Hall... Bring the police! ... What?... No, not in Greece - in Marlinspike Hall!

Drop that telephone, you!

Starlings bite? ... Hello?... Hello?...Starlings bite what? ...

Marlinspike, Captain! Marlinspike Hall!

What?... Martin's bike?... Hello?... Hello?... Thundering typhoons! What's going on?

Marlinspike Hall! ... Marlinspike!

Hello, Captain? Can you hear me? ... I'm at Marlinspike Hall! No, Marlinspike's the name!

What? ... What sort of game? ... Hello! He's rung off!

HELP! HELP!

That was Nestor's voice!

That's torn it! The telephone's broken!

There's only one thing to do - run for it - double quick!

If he's here he can't escape us...

By thunder! He's knocked out Nestor!

Where's he gone? Quick fool, tell us! Did he have time to use the telephone?

He did!

Who did he get?

He got me!

This is where I slip out . . .

Gently does it . . .

There! . . . There he goes! . . . He was hiding behind the door.

Little fiend, we'll get you, dead or alive!

Quick, old man, lend me your halberd.

Steady... they're coming!

This way out!

The front door just slammed. Get up, you two. He'll escape us...

Free at last!

There he goes!

Crumbs, they're after me again!

Missed! He's disappeared among the trees!

Fetch Brutus, Nestor! Quickly!

Brutus? Very well, sir!

What an enormous park: it's like a forest...

WOOF! WOOF!

Find him, Brutus! Find him!

Go on, find him! We musn't lose the scent.

Brutus!... Here Brutus!

WOOF! WOOF!

Saved!... What luck!

WOOF!
WOOF!

WOOF!
WOOF!

What shall I do?... If I run they'll let the dog go and I'll have them on my track. But if...

Yes, my mind's made up. I must risk everything!

We're nearly there; that barking isn't far off.

Whoops! That's it!

The joke's over, you gangsters! Hands up!

Now get up and start walking... Back to the house!

We can have a nice comfortable chat there while we wait for the police to arrive...

WOOF!
WOOF!

50

Where are they going? ... Oh, I see: that little wretch is taking care to put Brutus back in his kennel.

WOOF! WOOF!

That's that! And now, gentlemen, we'll go to the police-station!

They're coming back this way: they'll pass under the ground-floor windows. Perhaps there's some way...

Keep cool, Nestor!

Here they come! Careful, don't miss...

Nestor!

Oh, dear, I didn't hit him hard enough...

Now then, once more...

Oh dear!!

Got you this time, my young friend!

Come out here, Nestor, and bring some strong cord with you.

You, walk in front! I don't have to tell you - one false move and I'll shoot you like a dog!

! OW! Snowy!

Snowy! Good old Snowy!... You managed to find me!

Hands up!
Again?

Great snakes!... That sounds like the two Thomsons!
Hands up!

And there's Captain Haddock!... Hooray!
!

Ha, bully!... Ha, pirate!... Ha, pickled herring!

Captain! Look out, Captain!... What are you doing?

? | That's one for you, sycophant!

That thug had come round - he was just going shoot you...

Let me go!... I keep telling you - it's all a mistake: I'm not the one to arrest...

Ah, here come Thomson and Thompson... Hello.

It's this little ruffian, this little wretch who broke into the house and terrorized my masters; he's a real gangster, Mr. Detective...

It's true, Nestor acted in good faith. I heard his master say I was a criminal. Nestor believed it.

Then your masters are the criminals. Look what's left of my bottle of three-star brandy! It's all their fault!... They're gangsters!... dizzards!.. baboons!

And what's more, we have a warrant for their arrest.

My wallet! My wallet! It's incredible!

But your wallet's there...

That's just what's incredible: no one has stolen it!

By the way, what about that pickpocket?!... Have you managed to lay hands on him?

Not yet, but it won't be long now. ...

We got his name from the Stellar Cleaners: he's called Aristides Silk. We were just about to pull him in when we were ordered to arrest the Bird brothers, and here we are...

Quiet! Quiet! Listen to me!

Gentlemen, there has been a miscarriage of justice! This man is innocent, as Tintin said. Won't you take off these handcuffs... and let him go and fetch me another bottle of brandy?

There, my man, now you're free. And we'll use these handcuffs for your masters!

We'll follow you, Nestor. Don't forget: it's to be three-star!

Now, Captain, tell me how you came to be here.

Oh, yes... Right. Well...

Just after your telephone call — and I didn't und- erstand a word of that — someone rang up from the hospital...

... where they still had the little-birds-man. After hovering between life and death, he'd just come round and identified his attackers: the Bird brothers, antique dealers of Marlinspike Hall. It was only when I heard that name...

... that I understood what you meant on the telephone. There was no time to lose: I warned the police at once, and we rushed here ...

WHAM * OH!

WHAM OW!

? **?**

We shouldn't have left the police with those two gangsters!...

Look!... one's escaping!... there! He's just turned the corner!

He's the most dangerous of the two: he mustn't get away!

BRRRR BRRR

A car! That's a car starting up!

Road-hog!... Cyclone!... Bashi-bazouk!... Steamroller!

Too late! He's gone!

We'll take care of the other one later; let's go and help those two!

Wait: I'll give you a hand...

At last!.. Got it!

Now, my friend, I'm waiting for an explanation...

I'm saying nothing!

Perhaps you don't know that your victim recovered yesterday, and divulged your name..

Our victim? I...Barnaby wasn't dead!

Very well: I'd better tell you everything. When we bought this house, two years ago, we found a little model ship in the attic, in very poor condition...

The UNICORN?

Yes, and when we were trying to restore the model we came across the parchment: its message intrigued us. My brother Max soon decided it referred to a treasure. But it spoke of three unicorns; so the first thing was to find the other two... You know we are antique dealers. We set to work...

... We used all our contacts: the people who comb the markets for interesting antiques; the people who hunt through attics; we told them to find the two ships. After some weeks one of our spies, a man called Barnaby, came and said he'd seen a similar ship in the Old Street Market. Unfortunately, this ship had just been sold to a young man; Barnaby tried in vain to buy it from him.

Yes, we know the rest. It was Barnaby whom you ordered to steal my UNICORN. But because the parchment wasn't there, he came back and ransacked the place - again unsuccessfully. And then?

Then? Oh well, I'd better tell you the lot...

Barnaby came back empty-handed. Then he suddenly remembered the other man who'd been trying to buy the ship from you.

And next day he visited Mr. Sakharine, chloroformed him, and stole the third parchment...

That's right. But after he'd given it to us, he and Max quarrelled violently about the money we'd agreed he should have. Barnaby demanded more, but Max stuck to the original sum. Finally Barnaby went, furiously angry and saying we'd regret our meanness. When he'd gone, Max got cold feet: supposing the wretch betrayed us? We jumped into the car and trailed him; our fears were justified. We saw him speaking...

... to you. Panicking in case he'd given the whole game away, Max caught up with you in a few seconds, and shot Barnaby as he stepped into your doorway.

I understand so far: but tell me, why did you kidnap me?

We told you: to make you give up the two parchments you had stolen from us a few days after the shooting.

I see. But I couldn't have stolen them as I didn't know you existed! But I wonder... Perhaps it was...

Yes, perhaps it was Mr. Sakharine who took the two scrolls?

Hurrah! That's it!

At last! ...He's managed to get it off for me...

Come on, Captain, we'd better help this poor chap...

Ready! Steady! He-e-eave!

Whoops!

Captain, as soon as we return we'll see Mr. Sakharine. I'm sure he took the two scrolls...

Yes, we've only got one...

One! Great snakes! we haven't even got that! The Bird brothers took it! But we can get it back!

Give me back the parchment you stole from my room!

Give it back?... That's impossible... Max has it in his pocket!

Ring up the police-station at once; give them a description of Max Bird, and his car number - LX 188. Then we'll go straight back to town...

Right!

Next morning...

Now for Mr. Sakharine...

RRRING

Mr. Sakharine? He's gone away, young man. He won't be back for a fortnight.

He would be away! That doesn't make things any easier!

In the meantime I'll go and see the Thomsons. Perhaps they'll be able to tell me if they've found Max Bird...

Good morning. Are you going out?... I just came to ask you...

Sh! Mum's the word! Come with us!

Where are we going?

You'll soon see...

...and a few minutes later...

RAT TAT TAT TAT

Mr. Aristides Silk? Yes...

I arrest you in the name of the law! Arrest me?...

Yes, you! You are a thief, sir!...

A thief! Aristides Silk, retired civil servant: a thief! It's a mistake, gentlemen, a shocking mistake!

I'm sorry to interrupt you, Mr. Silk, but could you explain the meaning of all this?...

Property of R. Biggs pinched on 20-5-58

PAST

PICK POCKETS   WALLET-SNATCHERS

27-4-58   28-4-58

I...er, yes... Well, I... you see, I'm not a thief: certainly not! But I'm a bit of a... kleptomaniac. It's something stronger than I am: I adore wallets. So I... I... just find one from time to time. I put a label on it, with the owner's name...

...and I add it to my collection...

I venture to say, gentlemen, that this is a unique collection of its kind. And when I tell you that it only took me three months to assemble you'll agree that it's a remarkable achievement...

It's amazing! All these wallets in alphabetical order...

I wonder if by some extraordinary coincidence...

Hooray!

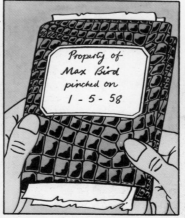
Property of Max Bird pinched on 1-5-58

And here are the two pieces of parchment!... Captain, Red Rackham's treasure is ours!

Goodbye! Don't forget to have a look under the letter T!

Under letter T?

Look under T? Why under T? ...

Good gracious! this belongs to me! ...

"Property of Thompson"! This is yours! ...

Property of Thomson... property of Thompson... Thomson... Thompson ...Thomson...Thompson...Thomson ...Thomson... Thompson... Thompson..

Next day...

Red Rackham's treasure is ours: it's easy enough to say. We've found two of the scrolls, I know, but we still haven't got the third ...

It looks as if...

RRRING
RRRING
RRRING

Hello?... Yes, it's me ... Good morning... What? you've arrested him?...

Not exactly, but thanks to the clues we gave, they managed to catch him trying to leave the country ...

What about the third parchment? ... Did you find it on him?...

Yes, he had it. We're bringing it along to you. But first we've got a little account to settle with this troublesome antique dealer...

Here, Thompson, hold my stick while I just deal with this gentleman...

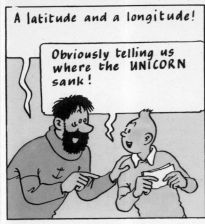

A latitude and a longitude!

Obviously telling us where the UNICORN sank!

Now, Captain... When do we leave on our treasure-hunt?

When do we leave? ... Er...

Let's see... first we need a ship... We can charter the SIRIUS, a trawler belonging to my friend, Captain Chester... Then we need a crew, some diving suits and all the right equipment for this sort of expedition... That will take us a little time to arrange. We'd better say a month. Yes, in a month we could be ready to leave.

Red Rackham's treasure will be ours!

But of course it won't be easy, and we shall certainly have plenty of adventures on our treasure-hunt... You can read about them in RED RACKHAM'S TREASURE

- HERGÉ -

HERGÉ

THE ADVENTURES OF TINTIN

RED RACKHAM'S
TREASURE

METHUEN CHILDREN'S BOOKS

LONDON

**Translated by Leslie Lonsdale-Cooper
and Michael Turner**

The TINTIN books are published
in the following countries :

Argentina :	JUVENTUD ARGENTINA,	Buenos Aires
Australia :	HICKS, SMITH & SONS,	Sydney
Belgium :	CASTERMAN,	Tournai
Brazil :	DISTRIBUIDORA RECORD,	Rio de Janeiro
Canada :	METHUEN,	Toronto
Denmark :	CARLSEN/IF,	Copenhagen
Egypt :	DAR AL MAAREF,	Cairo
Finland :	OTAVA,	Helsinki
France :	CASTERMAN,	Paris
Germany :	CARLSEN VERLAG,	Reinbek-Hamburg
Great Britain :	METHUEN,	London
Greece :	PEGASUS,	Athens
Iceland :	FJÖLVI,	Reykjavik
Indonesia :	INDIRA,	Djakarta
Iran :	PAT MARTY,	Teheran
Israel :	MIZRAHI,	Tel Aviv
Italy :	GANDUS,	Genoa
Japan :	SHUFUNOTOMO,	Tokyo
Mexico :	MARIN,	Mexico
Netherlands :	CASTERMAN,	Utrecht
New Zealand :	HICKS, SMITH & SONS,	Wellington
Norway :	SCHIBSTED,	Oslo
Peru :	DISTR. DE LIBROS DEL PACIFICO,	Lima
Portugal :	CENTRO DO LIVRO BRASILEIRO,	Lisbon
Singapore :	BOOKS FOR ASIA,	Singapore
South Africa :	HUMAN & ROUSSEAU,	Cape Town
Spain :	JUVENTUD,	Barcelona
Sweden :	CARLSEN/IF,	Stockholm
U.S.A. :	ATLANTIC -LITTLE, BROWN,	Boston